This book is the property of
Dr. LüToni Medaglia 1/14/07

This book is the property of
Dr. LüToni Medaglia

because life is beautiful

BEFORE I KNEW YOU
First Printing 2006

Text copyright 2006 by Shelley R. Lee
Illustrations copyright 2006 by Denise Lehman

Library of Congress Cataloging-in-Publication Data

International Standard Book Number 0-9786757-0-3

Cover: 1989 Drawing by Denise Lehman of Hannah R. Lee with Jesus
Layout & Design: Shelley R. Lee, Trevor M. Lee
Printed by Kings Time Printing Press in Hong Kong

Distributed by
Bowling Green Pregnancy Center
441 Frazee Ave. Suite A
Bowling Green, OH 43402
www.BeforeIKnewYou.com

BEFORE
I KNEW YOU

by Shelley R. Lee

Illustrated by Denise Lehman

It may seem like I've always known you
because I've been with you ever
since you can remember.

But there was a time before I knew you

when you were so very small that
Mommy didn't even know you were
there yet.

Inside Mommy
you started out smaller
than a grain of sugar.

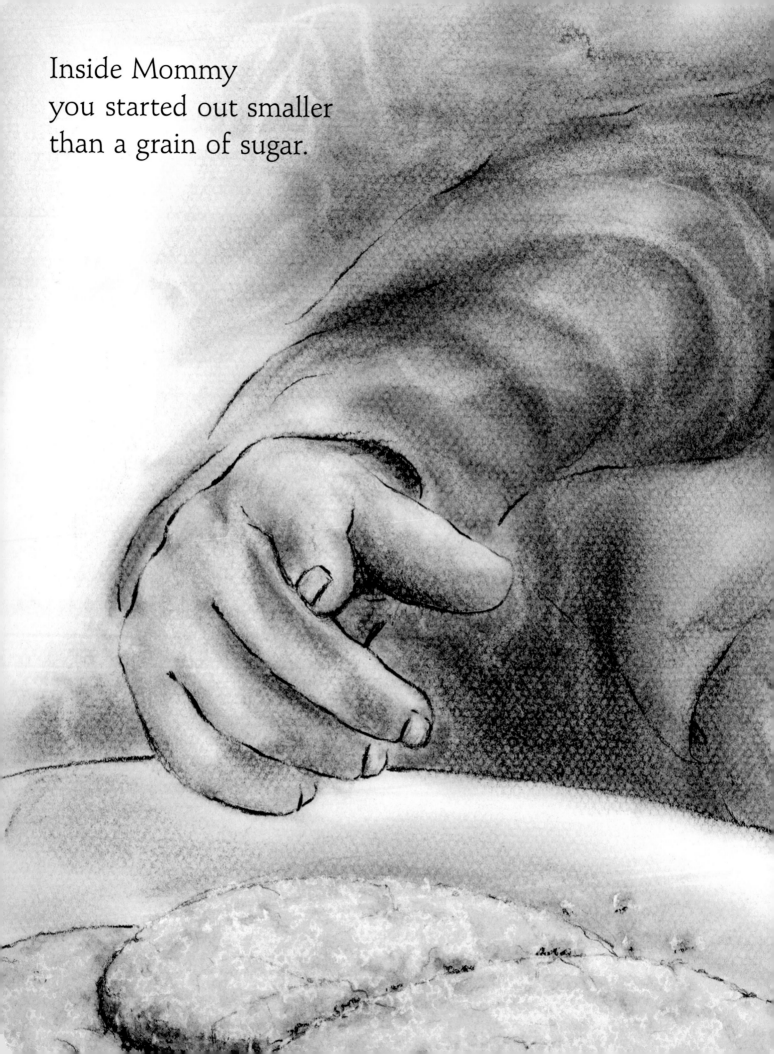

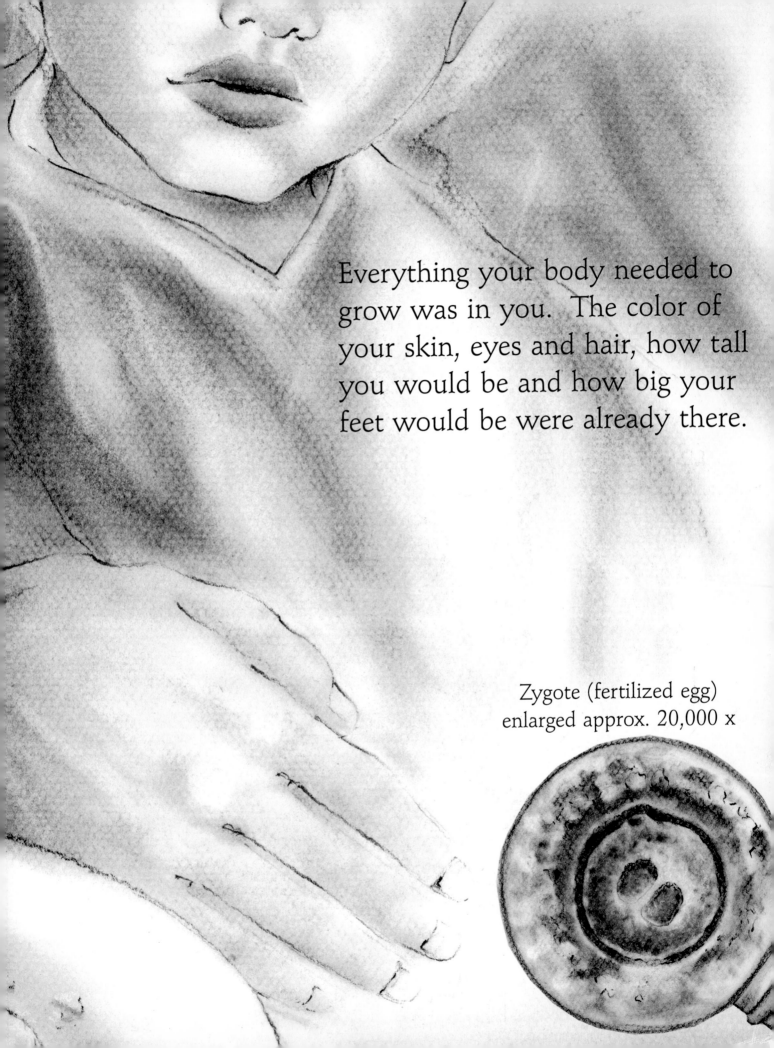

Everything your body needed to grow was in you. The color of your skin, eyes and hair, how tall you would be and how big your feet would be were already there.

Zygote (fertilized egg)
enlarged approx. 20,000 x

On the 21st day inside Mommy
your heart began to beat.

On the 28th day your backbone and muscles began forming. Your arms, legs, eyes and ears began to show.

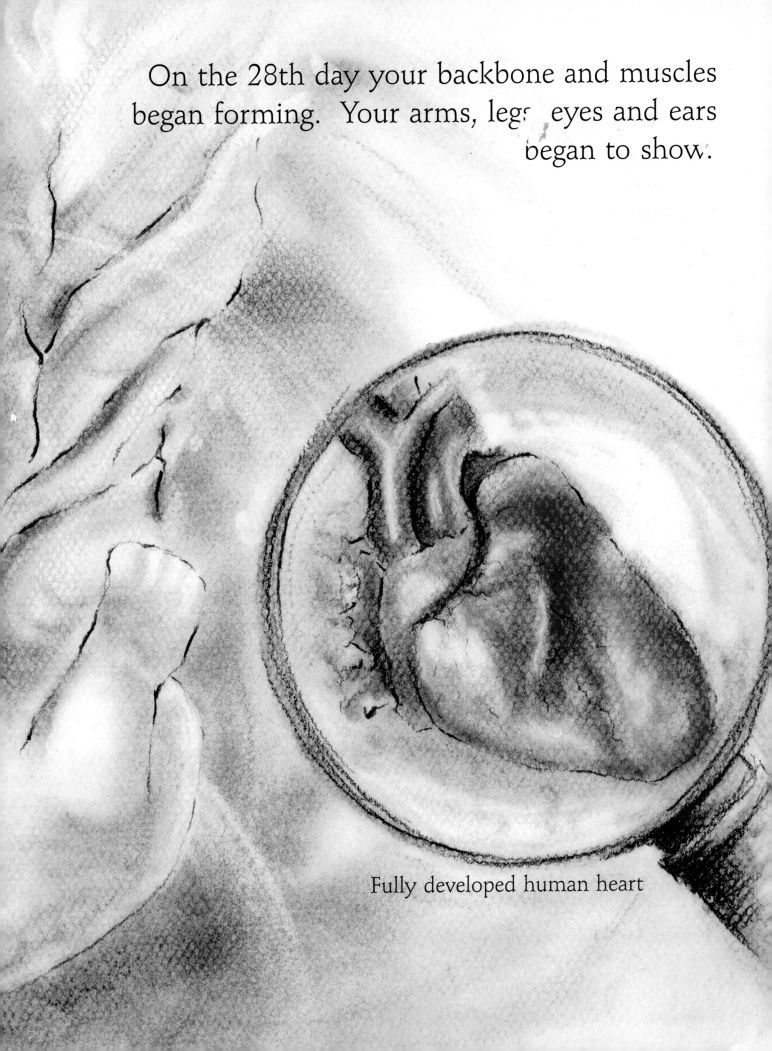

Fully developed human heart

On the 30th day (one month)
you were 10,000 times bigger than
you started out! Food and oxygen
are now passing from
Mommy to you.

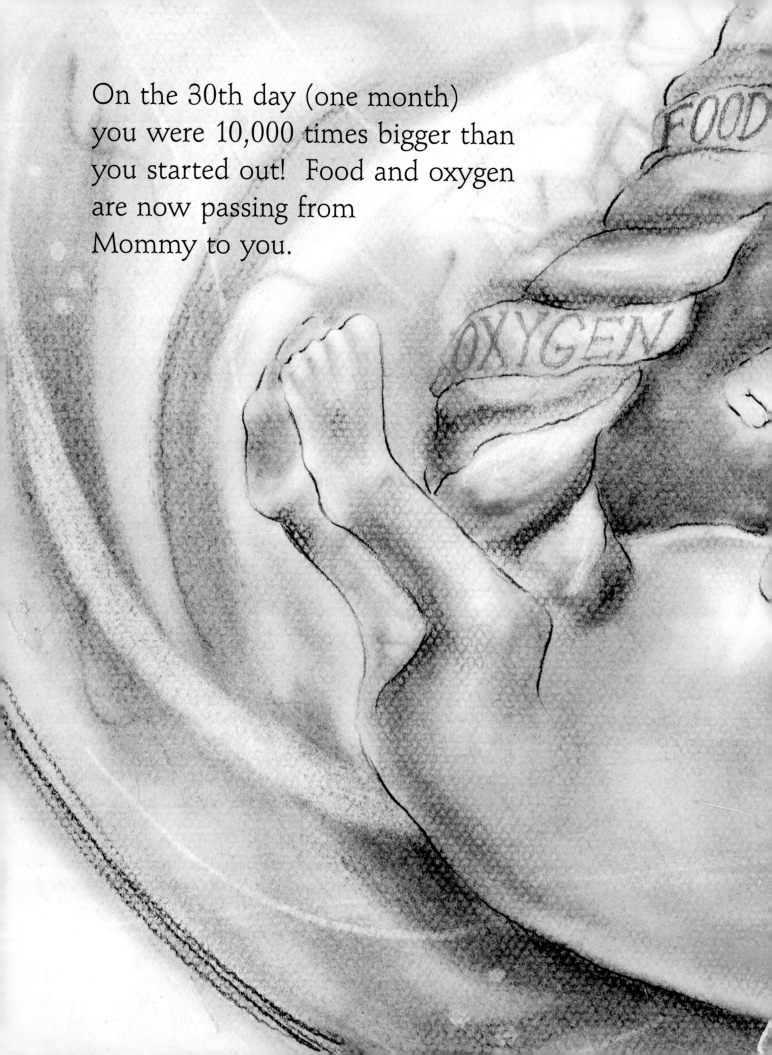

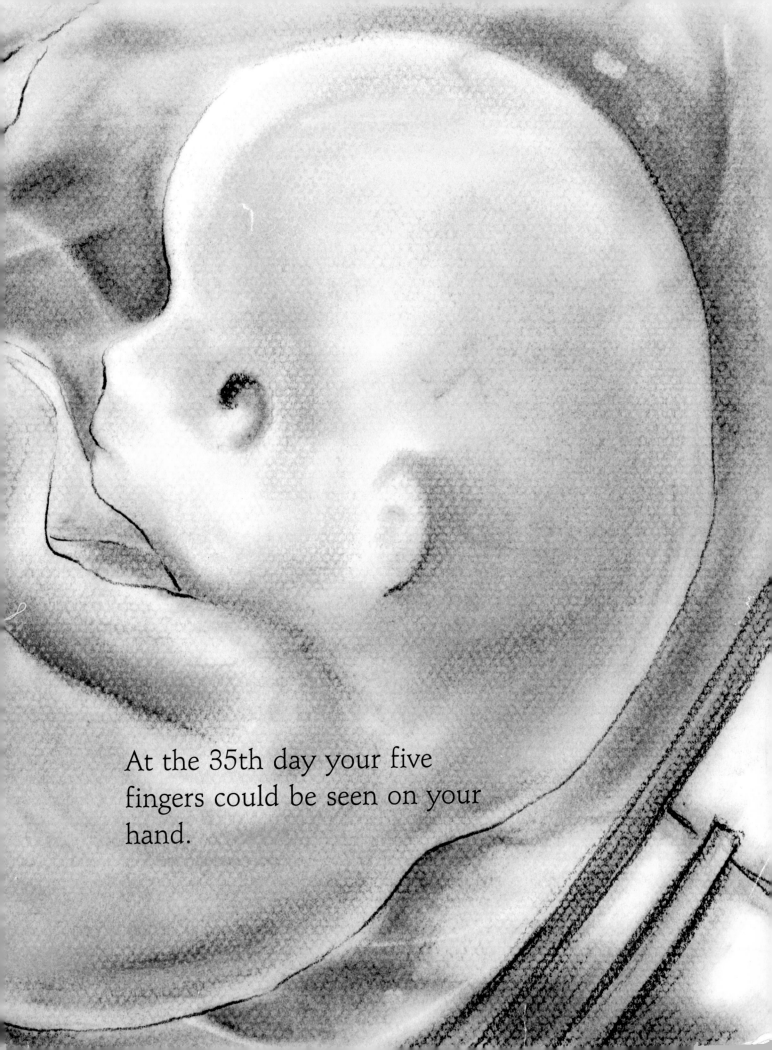

At the 35th day your five fingers could be seen on your hand.

On the 40th day brain waves
began to move through your brain.
You were starting to think.

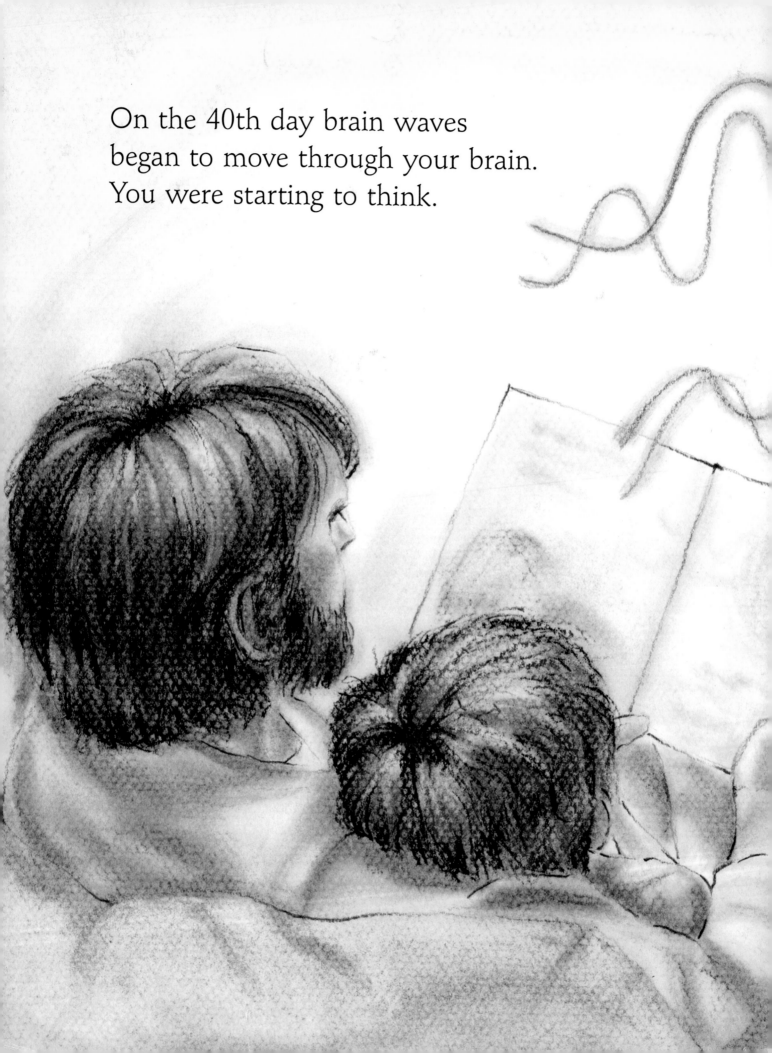

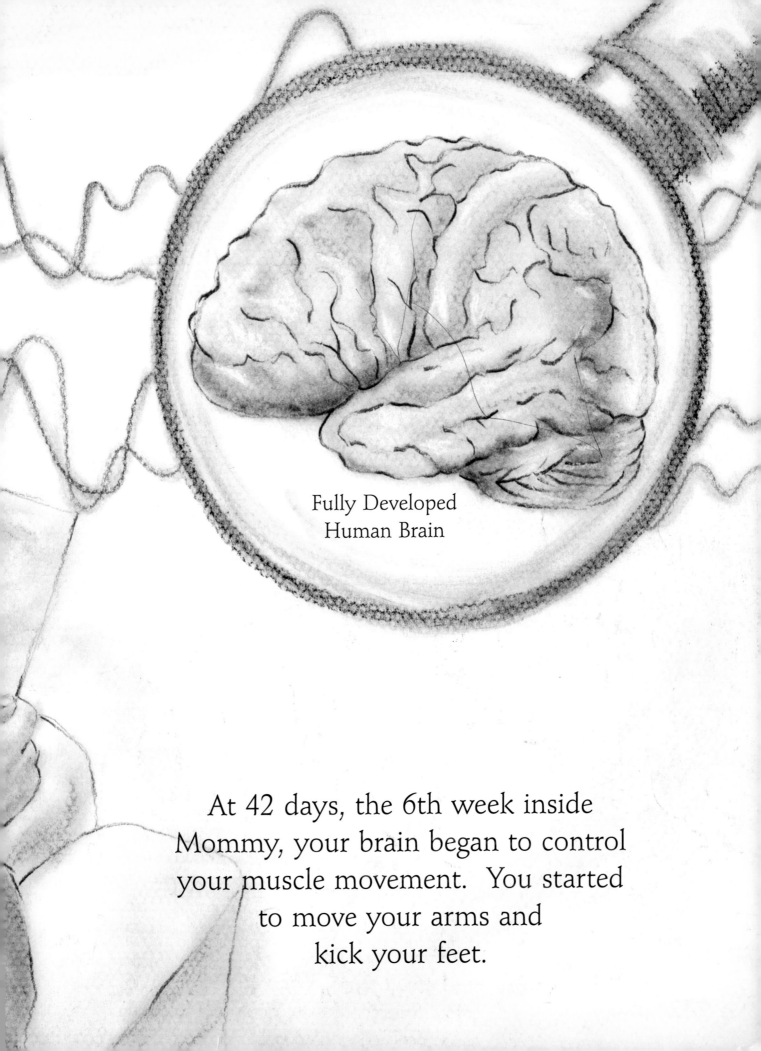

Fully Developed
Human Brain

At 42 days, the 6th week inside
Mommy, your brain began to control
your muscle movement. You started
to move your arms and
kick your feet.

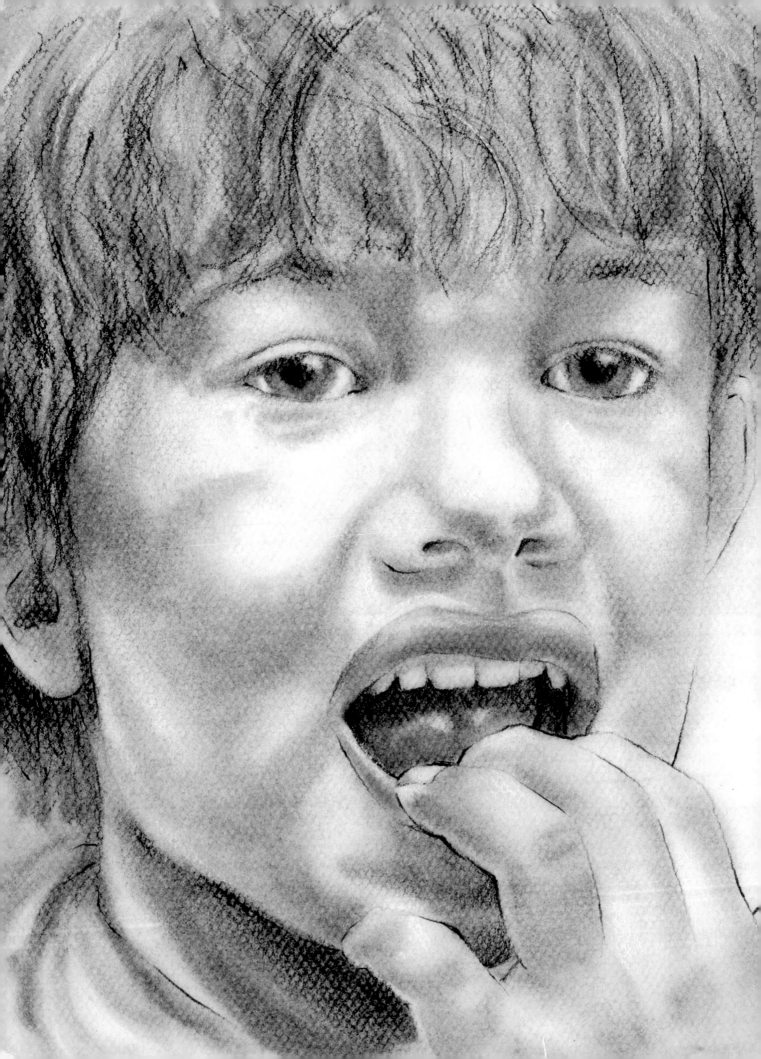

At the 7th week your jaw and teeth buds
formed. Soon after that your eyelids
sealed up to protect your developing
light sensitive eyes.

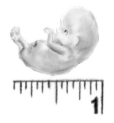

At week 8 (2 months) inside Mommy you
were a little more than an inch long.
Your body had everything that could be
found in a fully formed adult.

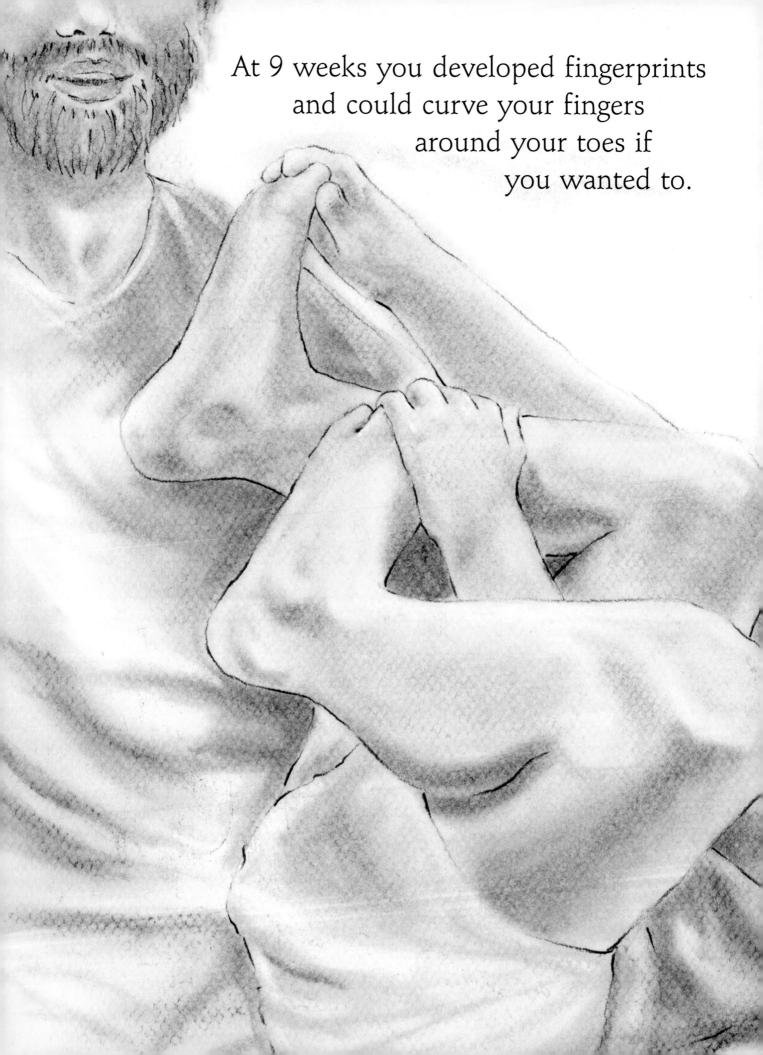

At 9 weeks you developed fingerprints
and could curve your fingers
around your toes if
you wanted to.

At 10 weeks you could swallow
and wrinkle your little forehead.

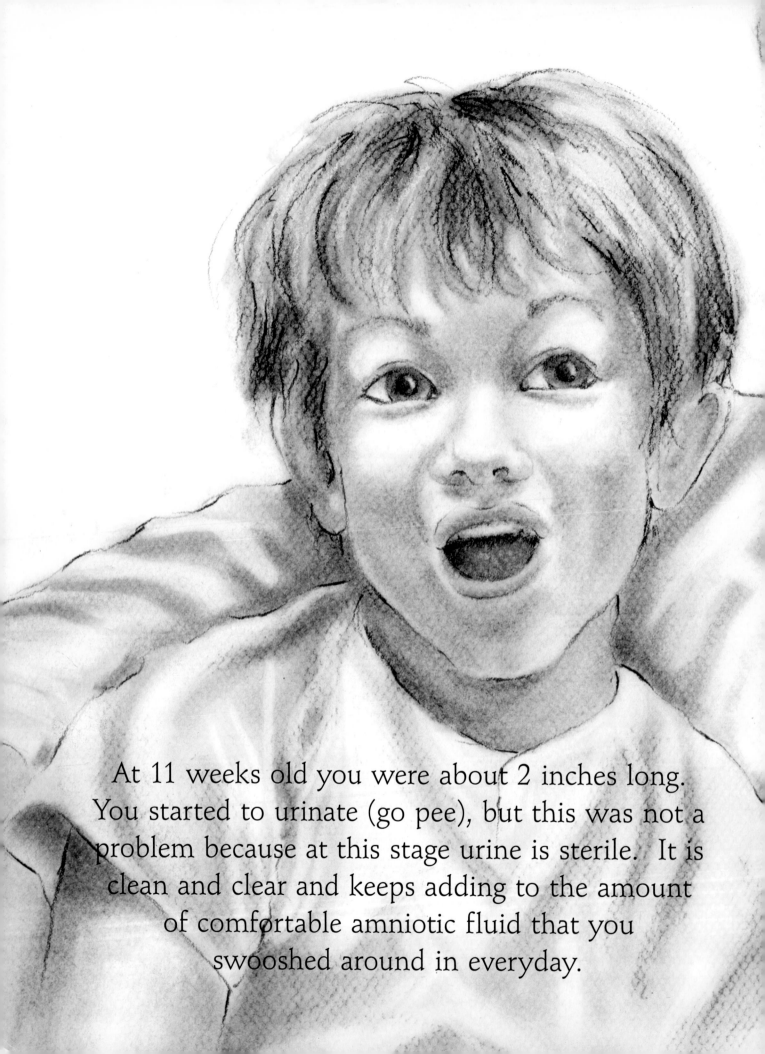

At 11 weeks old you were about 2 inches long.
You started to urinate (go pee), but this was not a
problem because at this stage urine is sterile. It is
clean and clear and keeps adding to the amount
of comfortable amniotic fluid that you
swooshed around in everyday.

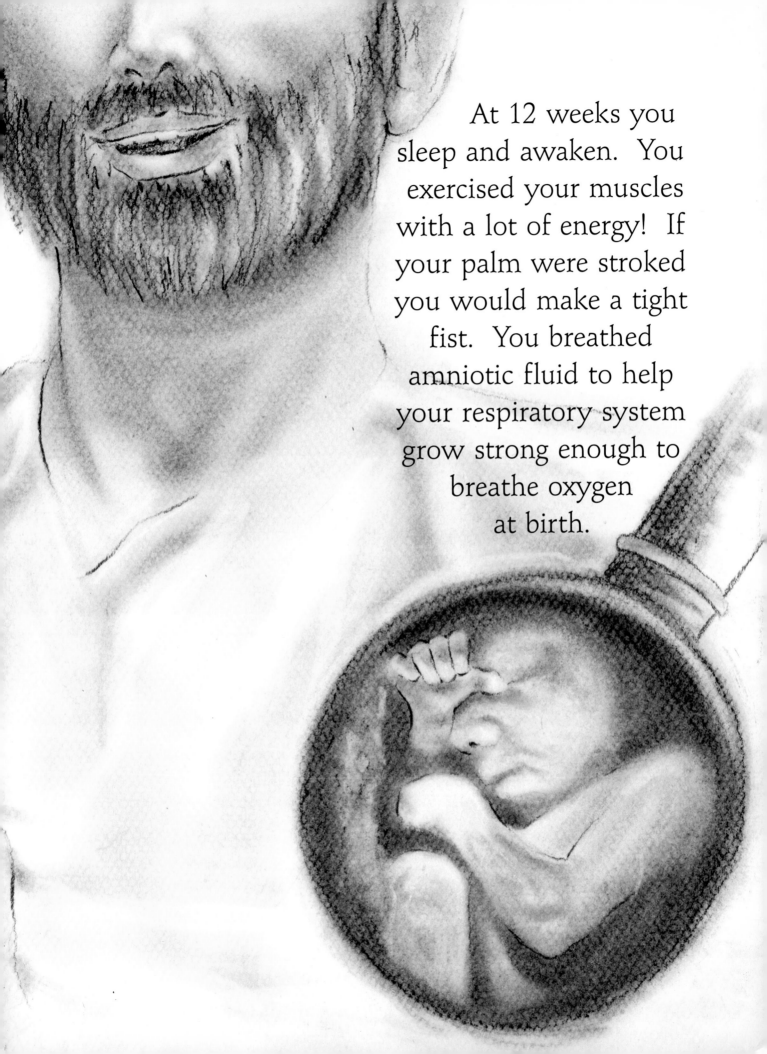

At 12 weeks you sleep and awaken. You exercised your muscles with a lot of energy! If your palm were stroked you would make a tight fist. You breathed amniotic fluid to help your respiratory system grow strong enough to breathe oxygen at birth.

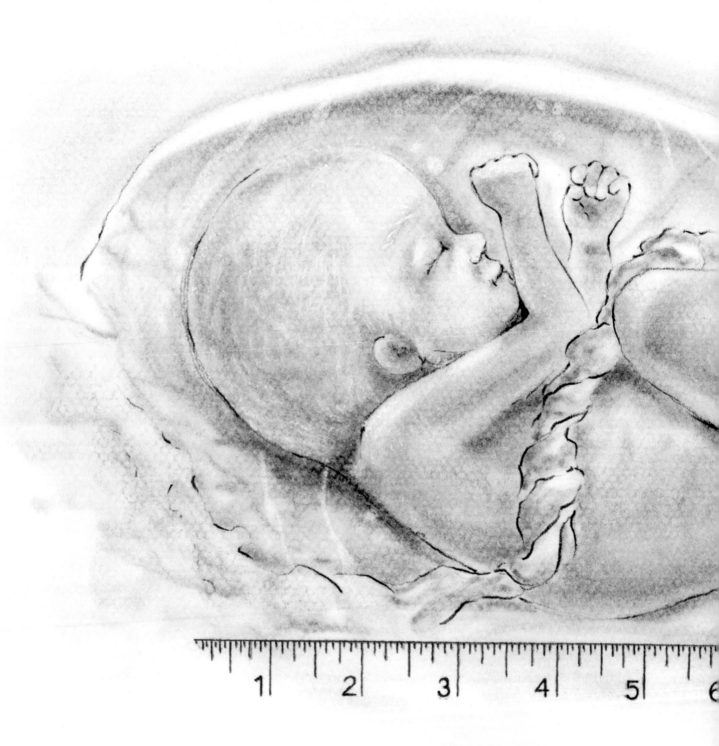

At 13 weeks you began to grow hair.

At 4 months old you had grown to a whopping 8 to 10 inches long in a few short weeks. Your ears began functioning and you heard Mommy's heartbeat, her voice and lots of other things outside, from your warm little world in the womb.

At 5 months you started
kicking, turning and even hic-
cupping. Mommy could feel
you bumping around
a lot!

The umbilical cord that sends nourishment
from Mommy to you, kept growing
thicker as blood flow increased to make
you stronger and bigger everyday.

At 6 months your face was a smaller version of what you'd look like as a newborn. You were gaining weight rapidly! Your bones were beginning to harden and your lungs were getting ready to breathe on their own.

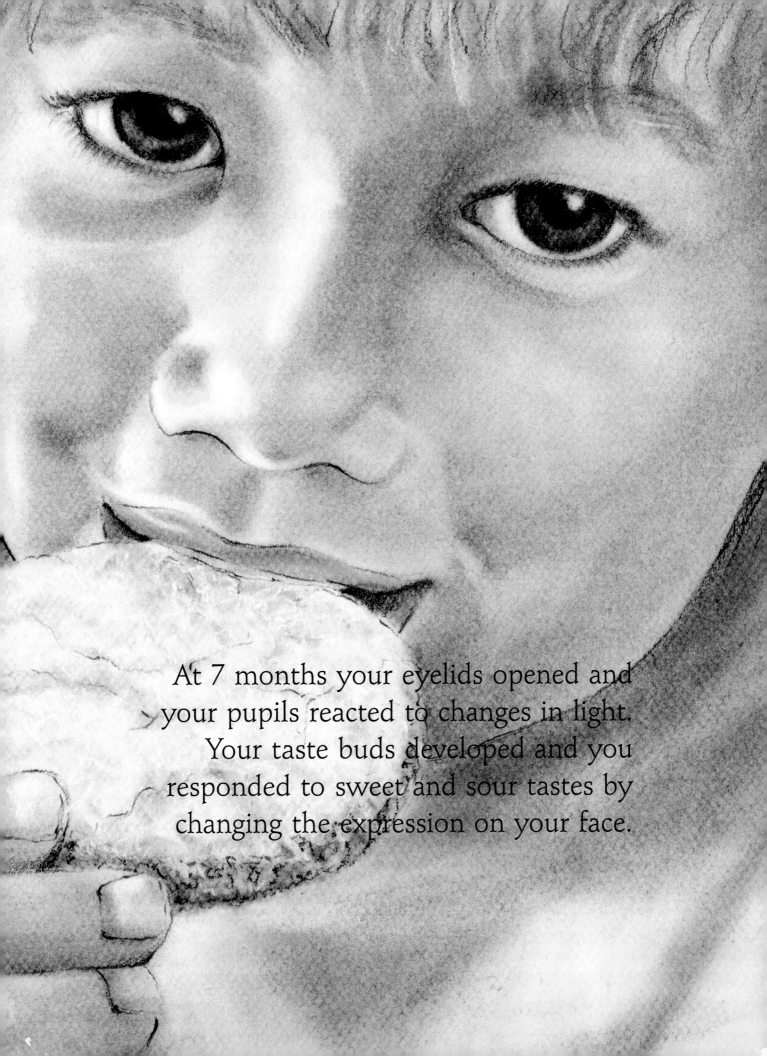

At 7 months your eyelids opened and your pupils reacted to changes in light. Your taste buds developed and you responded to sweet and sour tastes by changing the expression on your face.

At 8 months your brain was maturing and continued doing so long after you were born. Your arms and legs were becoming smooth and plump and your fingernails were growing so much that they probably needed trimming at birth.

At 9 months you were in the 40th week of development. You were running out of room inside Mommy! It was safe for you to be born anytime within the 9th month. Your arrival was anxiously awaited!

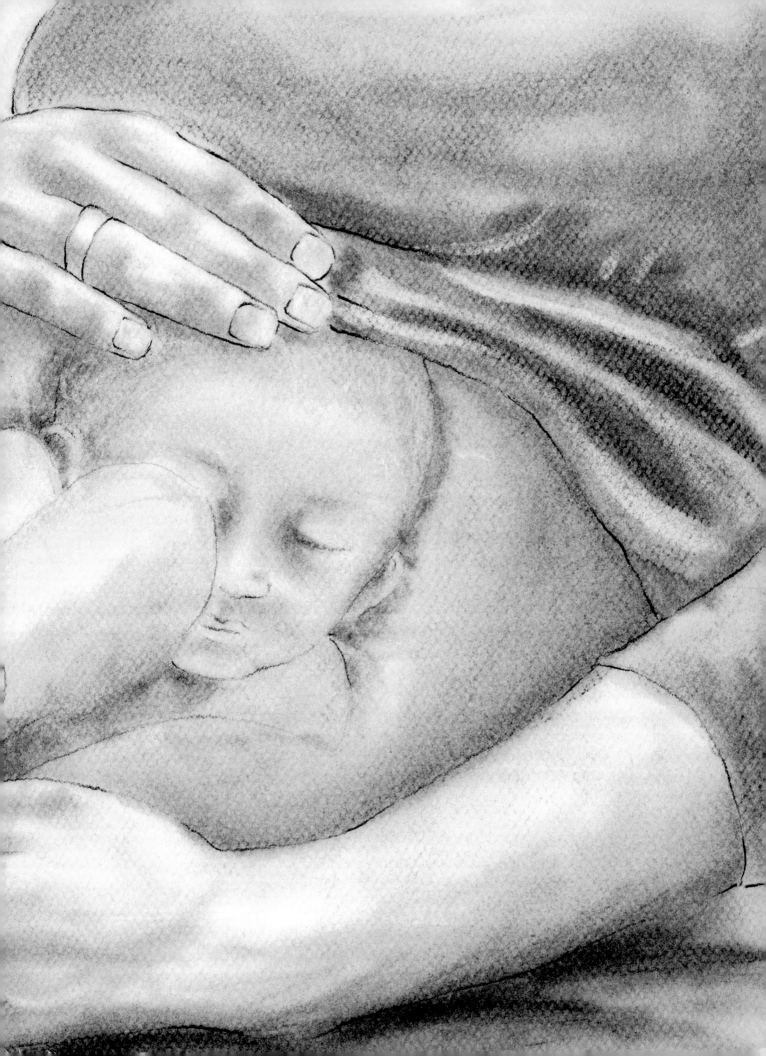

That was before we knew you and even
then, you were loved more
than you can imagine.
You
are the amazing person you
were meant to be.

About the Author

Shelley Lee is the director of the Bowling Green Pregnancy Center in Bowling Green, Ohio. She attended Grand Valley State University in Michigan where she earned a bachelor's degree in public relations as well as psychology. She attains that no matter where she has had the privilege to work or travel, no matter what dreams may have come and gone (or stayed), there is no greater privilege than to parent. She spent the first 14 years of parenthood as a domestic engineer (a.k.a. stay-at-home-mom). Shelley and her husband Dave, a teacher and wrestling coach, live in rural NW Ohio with their four fun teenage boys. A picture of their infant daughter Hannah whom they lost to SIDS is pictured on the cover.

About the Illustrator

Denise Lehman is a freelance illustrator with a bachelor of fine arts degree from Kendall College of Art and Design in Grand Rapids, Michigan. She has enjoyed working from home on a plethora of design projects over the past 20 years. She resides outside Charlotte, North Carolina with her husband Tim, a furniture designer, and their four thriving sons. Denise first met Shelley in high school in Saline, Michigan where they spent many semesters in art class together.